# Brita and Time

Written by

L. Priyadharshini

Illustrated by

Kavingyar Gokila Velusamy

**Ukiyoto Publishing**

All global publishing rights are held by

**Ukiyoto Publishing**

Published in 2023

Content Copyright © L. Priyadharshini
**ISBN** 9789360160623

*All rights reserved.*
*No part of this publication may be reproduced, transmitted, or stored in a retrieval system, in any form by any means, electronic, mechanical, photocopying, recording or otherwise, without the prior permission of the publisher.*

*The moral rights of the author have been asserted.*

*This is a work of fiction. Names, characters, businesses, places, events, locales, and incidents are either the products of the author's imagination or used in a fictitious manner. Any resemblance to actual persons, living or dead, or actual events is purely coincidental.*

*This book is sold subject to the condition that it shall not by way of trade or otherwise, be lent, resold, hired out or otherwise circulated, without the publisher's prior consent, in any form of binding or cover other than that in which it is published.*

*This title is produced in Association with Pachyderm Tales*

**www.pachydermtales.com**

# ACKNOWLEDGEMENT

I whole heartedly thank,

Mohanasundari Jaganathan,

(Managing Director of Sharp Electrodes Pvt Ltd)

for funding this project.

Without her, this book would not be possible!

This book was a part of workshop conducted in our college, NGM College Pollachi and Pachyderm Tales.

I whole heartedly thank our management, our teachers and HOD of English Dept, NGM as well as Suja Mam for this initiative.

Hello friends!
Meet Brita from London. She is nine years old. She lives a happy life with her family in a small city located in Sheer.

Her father works as a co-operate company officer. Her mom is a house wife. Brita is a single child and she feels sad about not having siblings.

Anyways it's a Sunday and Sunday is always a special day for Brita. She used to visit the park on all Sundays and spend time playing with Smith, who is her best friend.

Suddenly, Brita's mom called her from the kitchen *"Brita… don't waste your time. Go and start your preparations for the examinations."*

Brita sat as if she never minded.

*"No, I can't. I have to spend my whole day on the playing field with Smith. He will be waiting for me."*

*"Please understand mom. I can't learn today. It's a holiday. Please, I can't"* she pleaded.

She thought hard about finding a way to escape her exams.

*"How can I escape from my exam? I could not prepare anything and it's too late already."*

# Brita and Time

On her exam day, she went home in her uniform and bag. But she did not go to school.

Instead, she went to the park and enjoyed herself with the birds and animals there.

*"How does the bee look this beautiful?"* she asked herself.

*"Will you play with me little one?"* Brita asked the bee.

*"No, I can't, I have to roam around and collect the honey."* The bee replied.

*"Will you play with me, mother bird?"* She asked the bird.

*"No, I can't play with you. I need to feed my kids."* The bird refused.

# Brita and Time 13

*"Oh God, no one likes me. No one cares for me. I am all alone. Nobody plays with me."* She cried.

Brita went near the river and she saw a fish. *"Hello little fish. Will you play with me? No one is there for me. Please play with me…"* she pleaded again.

*"I don't have time. I have to take care of myself and my fingerlings."* replied the fish.

*"Will you play with me?"* Brita asked Crocodile.

*"No one is there to play with me."*

The crocodile replied, *"No, I don't have time. I have to search for food and fill my stomach."*

In a last attempt, Brita asked the tree, "*Will you play with me?*"

"*No, I cannot. I have a lot of work to do. I have carbon dioxide to be converted into oxygen so humans can live longer.*", the tree replied.

In the evening, Brita called Smith and asked her to come to the park.

She was a smart girl. She said "*I have an exam tomorrow. I can't come to the park. Please don't misunderstand me.*"

Brita sadly said, "*No one loves me. No one needs me.*"

# Brita and Time 23

Brita asked flower,

*"How are you happy all the time? What makes you happy?"*

"It is not about a long life for me; I enjoy every moment of my life. So, I am happy." Flower said.

Brita thought, *"I can play today and work later."*

Brita walked to the playground and played alone. She kept murmuring, *"No one is there for me."*

Brita slept at night. In her dreams, she saw the lives of animals, trees, crocodiles, and many more organisms.

She also saw them enjoying their lives to the fullest.

The next day, Brita headed to school.

*"I did not touch my books for the exam; all the students were writing well. How will I write?"* Brita wondered.

That evening, she kept thinking, *"No one will assist me, no one will come with me. My close friend too cheated."*

Brita wasted time by thinking about the mistake that she had made.

# Brita and Time 31

On Friday, there was the distribution of paper in the class.

Brita was trembling and thought to herself, *"I will surely have scored low marks. My mom would kill me if she comes to know of this."*

Brita exclaimed *"Oh No! I am in the worst situation."*

# Brita and Time 33

She got the paper and went home to disclose her marks to her mother.

*"Mom, the answer papers were distributed today. My score is…"* She paused.

Brita's mom, took away her papers and was shocked. *"I never expected this result."* said Soma.

Soma was frustrated. *"Don't go to playground from now on. You should spend all your time learning. Am I clear?"*

*"No, I can't. I am not interested in reading or learning. I get bored when I open a book. I have to play with my friends."* Said Brita.

# Brita and Time

Smith had scored good mark. So, her mom appreciated Smith.

*"I also want appreciation from my mom, like Smith."* She felt bad.

Ego made her work hard.

*"I also want to score good marks next time."* she thought to herself.

Brita did not waste any single second from then on.

Brita motivated herself, *"I can do it, I can do it."*

After a month, Brita came back home having written her examinations and told her mom,

*"I have done my examination well!"*

When the answer sheets were distributed, Brita proudly said

*"I am the happiest person in the world. I have scored good marks."*

Brita went to her mom and said in a husky tone, *"I have received my paper. I have scored..."* she paused.

Soma stood, worried.

"99%", Brita disclosed. Her face was filled with full confidence when she said that.

Soma congratulated her daughter, *"Well done my dear. Keep it up. I am proud of you."*

Brita was very happy. She shared the happy news with everyone, like birds, bees, flowers, trees and crocodiles.

# Brita and Time

# The Author

L. Priyadharshini is currently pursuing a degree in English literature at the undergraduate level. When her mother, a teacher, read devotions and stories about kings, she grew up listening to them. In childhood, she read more books and would narrate them to her schoolmates at prayer. She would imagine things in her mind and draw them on paper. It was JK Rowling's Harry Potter that inspired her to write this story. A fantasy and thriller writer, she enjoys writing stories in these genres.

## The Illustrator

Kavingyar Gokila Velusamy has completed her M.A.,B.Ed. and M.Phil., and is currently working at Maharishi International School. She holds the Authorship of three poetry books titled Kaatru Vaasitha Kavithai, Vavval Thootathu thalaikeel Maram, and Neem Fragrance Throughout.

www.ingramcontent.com/pod-product-compliance
Lightning Source LLC
LaVergne TN
LVHW041638070526
838199LV00052B/3436